Addiction and the New Dream

Addiction and the New Dream by George Harold Clowers, Jr.

© 2013 There Is This Place by George H. Clowers, Jr.

© The Case for Larry Fleming by George H. Clowers, Jr.

ALL RIGHTS RESERVED

This is a work of fiction, any resemblance to places or persons, living or dead is coincidental.

Cover Art by Deborah A. Clowers

ADDICTION AND THE NEW DREAM

Admittedly I have a pointed view of addiction and recovery, I am a recovering dope fiend of thirty-eight years, and a retired substance use disorder counselor who practiced for thirty years. Briefly, I have enough skeletons in my closet to fund medical research for a year, and enough experience with criminals to write another crime novel. Turn on any media source to get the details I wish not to discuss, but I lived them as well!

My first novel, The Case for Larry Fleming, spells out the racial, political, and business use of technology present in 2014, the year I wrote it. One of the central characters implores the principle to tell them about the 'New Dream', that is the major premise of Dr. King's era had been achieved so what was next? Of course it is an easy autopsy now due to the recent election here in America, but there has to be more nuance. Simply put, how has a certain level of degeneration become the premise of today's central governing theme, and how has the present state of addictive behavior, whether with substances, or gambling, become the driver of financial wellbeing? I offer this excerpt to explore the obvious and not so obvious causes for dysfunction and possible ways to hear that soaring poetry again!

Addiction and the Old Social Dream

The bus stopped a block from the building and when Larry walked toward it he recognized an elementary school friend, Rita Owens, sitting on a bench under a covered bus stop. She was plainly dressed in shorts and a blouse, hair fluffed in a short afro style. Her eyes darted left and right as if she were waiting on someone, or afraid of someone. Larry thought to speak, or pass by without any acknowledgement, thinking that she probably wouldn't remember him anyway as she didn't seem present. Almost without her permission, as he got to within eight feet of her, he spoke her name from years ago, "Rita Owens."

She looked at him, as if from afar, sensing that he was okay, and knowing that he was okay, she responded, "Bishop. Rita Bishop. Miss Owens died several years ago."

She licked her lips and touched the middle of her chest, just over the heart, and repeated, "Bishop. Rita Bishop. Miss Owens died several years ago."

He looked at her, not knowing what to say, or do. He wanted to be polite but wasn't sure what was the next right action to take.

"You know the dream is dead; so, you need another dream. No one has said that. Stuck in the past. New dream, what it means. New dream." She spoke as if before a camera, clear, and with passion.

"You know the dream; you know the dream. They will ask you one day, and you will know the dream."

"Drugs, mental illness," he thought.

"Rita, my name is Larry..." Before he could complete the sentence, she began, "Fleming. Larry Fleming. Good boy. Got into those drugs and alcohol. Sex with everybody. Jail. Junkie man, alcoholic, dope fiend. Hoe. I saw you on TV, and the good boy returned. Good man now. No drugs, no alcohol. God boy. Good boy. Frankie overdosed last year. Kenny too. Ronnie Brown been in jail 12 years. Maureen wanted to come visit you, but she was going to trick you. She dead. My uncle is clean now, Johnny too. They married. Two men, but that's okay. How ya mama n 'em? They say I'm crazy. That's okay. I live back there."

She pointed to a spot 200 yards east of the building, past an open, park like area with nice trees and shrubbery.

"Not in the woods. Daddy left me the house. The men, the ones who made the Mears building new wanted to buy it. Then wanted to take it when I wouldn't sell. "Thirty thousand," they said, "Thirty thousand." Where I'm gone live, they didn't say? Daddy had worked for some people who helped me keep the house. Money now for the rest of my life. Kept daddy's house. Larry the counselor, good man now, new dream, new dream now."

"Rita," Larry spoke.

"I'm going now. You go to work. New dream, new dream. You tell them."

With that she stood, walked past Larry, and didn't look back.

SET UP

Thomas Robinson learned about computers on the Tang machines back in 1974. Quadratic equations and linear programming came easily to him and working in the Decision Mathematics Department gave him access to brilliant minds and high energy trials. Dr. Leopard, department head, was patient with him, and so clear in his explanations. Drs. Peters and Banner allowed him to read their work, and he saw their calculations as a bridge to mechanical applications.

He went to work for the Atlanta Police Department in 1978 and seemed to have an innate ability to project intuition and probability onto encounters with the public. His formulated thoughts per second were such that he saved a few lives, cops, and potential victims, by sensing intent, or lack thereof, versus a real threat. One case that stands out was the night he and three other detectives rode up on Simpson and Ashby and noticed Gary and Ken Hughley standing around slinging dope. They had files on their activities the past two years and neither warranted much attention, although Gary was moving into a crime level that was bigger than just his nickel and dime hustling to support his habit. He was carrying guns now, and his friends were moving ounces at a time.

When Thomas exited the unmarked police car and chased after him he figured Gary was either armed, or at least had a syringe with needle on him. Thomas knew from reports today, from six stores, that Gary was involved in the theft of at least 90 pairs of sunglasses, his primary hustle these days. When Gary ran past Kenny, who threw 16 glassine bags into the air and turned left behind Nate's Hot Dog Store, he started to reach for his right leg pants cuff. Thomas could see that and so as he chased and turned the corner behind him he could see Gary's arm moving downward, then relax as if he'd thrown something atop the building. As Thomas drew his weapon a split-second decision was on him, is he armed, or was that something else? Fortunately for both Gary turned, with hands above his head, as Thomas had already decided not to shoot. That is when he got the idea for Weapons Eye Sync and was able to 'see' how valuable it would be if law enforcement had a device that could tell them if, and with what type of weapon subjects had on them, and their level of intention to do harm from at minimum ten yards away. He developed a basic concept, and made some drawings, and acquired a patent, # 661454332190. Ten years later he left the police force, took a job at Hobe Phone Company as a Systems Flow Designer, and that is where he met, and became familiar with the work of Bruce Walker, who had come over from Atlanta Scientific as a System Performance Analyst. They worked together on the company's top five projects for eight years and were then disbursed to top secret jobs in either research or training for the next twelve years. They retired from there in June 2008.

*

Funny how a movement affects an area, and an area affects a movement. The hardscrabble, blue-collar nature of the area near the Mears building had become home to the homeless, playground for the tricksters, and a focus for the aimless. The Atlanta Crackers baseball field was long gone, the Army recruiting office boarded up, and drunks were everywhere. Yet, there was a glamour to it all, a halo of night lights, clothes, and artist not yet distinguished, 24-hour eating places, and flop houses for the girls. The races had merged, and were getting to know each other, and north side businesses still paid the bills. Achievement mattered, and rural attitudes shaped the burgeoning urban landscape, "Yes sir, and No ma'am," could still be heard, and dating for pleasure was often the norm. High school and cars would state the obvious, compact, or large still meant something. The creeks and trussells and railroad tracks defined the places you should not go, or better yet, you had to explore. Cathy and Jeanie would come outside, cigarettes and wine could be bought, another day, another time.

*

Larry's ego wanted to present a better front even though his office was tasteful, with modern art and furnishings purchased by Darlene that could be resold later if necessary. Larry was a good counselor. He was well respected, but felt small at times because he, even as a young boy, thought that all his play mates had a dollar more than he had, that they went places, and did things, while he seemed always to be just out and about, running around, playing sports, spending money given to him by his aunts. He didn't seem to know how to make money like his uncles, but he cut the grass, or cleaned off roofs, painted houses and inside rooms. People knew they could depend on him, even as his bad years progressed he could be called on for small repairs and jobs the other young folks were not doing, at least in his neighborhood.

"Come in. Mr. Henson?"

"Yes, hi, Wallace Henson. Good morning. Good to meet you. Nelson spoke highly of you."

"Thank you. Yes, come on in, have a seat."

Wallace was having second thoughts about all of this. Maybe he was overreacting to his latest drinking spree, but his business woes were very real and foreboding. He thought he'd overpaid for the Weapons Eye Sync device and had borrowed way too much to finance the deal. Sure, the return potential was enormous, but he felt that his management skills were not strong enough to take the company to the next level. He would have to confide more in Jake about the deal but didn't want to corrupt the young man any more than he had already. Wallace thought he knew the racial politics and thought he could avoid the consequences of what Mr. Robinson's true motives were for the device's future. So, coming to talk to an older, black counselor from Atlanta, Georgia seemed appropriate on many levels.

"How is Nelson these days?" Larry asked, taking a seat, then gesturing towards a bottle of water and coffee pot. "Water, coffee?"

"No thanks," Wallace responds. "He's not well. Late-stage cancer. Bad."

Larry places his face in his upturned hands. "Well," he says under his breath.

They both shift in their chairs, eye one another with caution, let out a deep breath, then Larry asks him, "What can I do for you?"

Wallace was taken aback by the question, expecting more small talk about their mutual friend.

"Well, I'm not sure. I know you're primarily an addiction counselor, and I do have some issues there, but I have some other needs that may be related or not. Issues around business and social consciousness. I may have done something to hurt a lot of people where I wanted to be helpful. Good motive, potentially bad results."

"My general consults are $400.00. Then we'll see where we go from there."

"Sure, fine. Do I pay you now?"

"Let's get that out of the way first."

Wallace writes him a check for the amount, Larry offers a receipt. "That won't be necessary," Wallace says.

"You were born and raised here I understand?" Wallace asks.

"Yeah, sure. 1953. Grady Baby."
"What does that mean?"
"It means my roots are deep here."
"And you, where are you from?"
"New York actually. Just outside the city. Upper middle, neat, comfortable."
"Family?"
"Okay, let me tell you what's really going on," Wallace exhorts, and begins to sweat. "Those bastards want to kill me! But I want to get them first, business wise I mean. They look good on TV. Talking all that stuff. Chumps!" He's breathing heavily now, looking around the room, restless. He gets up, walks over to the table, and grabs the bottle of water. Screws the top off and returns to his seat. "I'm sorry. I messed up. Those bastards."

He takes a gulp of water, and looks directly at Larry, and asks, "You got something to drink around here?"

###

Larry walked up the two flights of stairs for his 11 o'clock massage with Teresa. He felt good that he didn't have any major body ailments that needed work. It had been a year and a few months since he emptied Aunt Cadelia's house to prepare for sale. He'd wrenched his right shoulder moving a refrigerator, strained both knees moving old metal desks, wooden boards, and shelving from the basement, and had fallen down the front porch steps moving a four-drawer filing cabinet, breaking the big toe of his left foot. Golf had stressed his lower back and clearing bushes and trees at his house had aggravated his whole body, especially inflaming the shoulders, forearm, and knees. His left heel showed signs of plantar fasciitis, and his feet generally hurt all day. OTC anti-inflammatory medications had kept him going, but four tablets a day were doing harm to his stomach, causing him to overeat. He'd not had a massage in six months and most of the ailments had healed so he looked forward to today's session.

Teresa, already a full-sized black woman at 5'8" 180lbs. looked as if she'd gained weight, sitting at the front desk, shoulders and face much fuller since the last time he saw her. She welcomed him warmly, seeming to not remember him, having to glance at her appointment book before speaking further, "Larry?"

"Yes. How are you?"

"Good. It's been a while," she speaks.

"Yes."

"Come on back."

She gets up and leads him down a short hallway saying, "Room 3."

"On the left?"

"No, on the right."

She gestures there, and he goes into the room.

The massage table was neatly wrapped with a sheet, and the top blanket folded back. The support pillow for the knees was evident, and the room was comfortably warm. The lighting was soft and gentle on the senses, just like the music.

"Go ahead and get ready, face down first," she offered. "I'll be back shortly."

"Okay," he responds.

Larry put his phone on silent, removes his tee and over shirt, put his socks in his shoes, right to right, left to left, and pushes them under the chair. He removes his pants, folding the clothes on the chair before sitting on the table. He slowly leaned sideways, then face down, positioning his face in the cradle, and gently shifting his face and body to get comfortable. It took several times to get his face comfortable, and to move his legs and arms to a resting position. He casually thought how good this felt and blinked his eyes a few times before closing them. Teresa returned in three minutes, just before Larry was beginning to question to himself how long it would be before she returned. She gently tapped on the closed door and came in, not hearing his response.

"Ready?" she had asked.

She moved to his left side and asked, "What are we working on today?"

"Just a general massage with some attention to my right shoulder," he answered.

She walked around the massage table, turned to the short, square cabinet that housed her supplies, picked out a jar of cream, and opened it. She asked if the room, blanket, and pad felt okay; he said yes. She then stepped backwards, then moved towards him, pushing his body at various points, waist, legs, hips, arms, shoulders. She touched his feet and jostled his ankles. She used her fingers on his back, pushing, sensing, probing, as Larry's mind became more active.

He thought of his last counseling session, and whether the guy would ever get honest about how much he drinks. He knew from past experiences that in a group setting it usually took about four sessions, but in individual people could minimize for weeks, choosing to talk about peripheral problems because they didn't have the benefit of older group members who were more comfortable with the process.

As the massage progressed Larry was able to mentally satisfy a few techniques to use for his next two clients later in the day, a lawyer, and a businessman. Teresa had touched a couple of sensitive areas, but generally there were no 'ouhwee' moments. He acknowledged to himself how powerful she was, yet, with just the right amount of force.

When she was nearing the end of the hour Larry asked if she had refined some of her previous techniques, observing that she seemed more in command of her huge talents.

"Oh," she paused, "Thanks. We do have to take classes to maintain our licenses. I like the hands-on classes, not just online, which we can have one half of. Thanks, I appreciate that," she responded.

"Oh yeah, my whole body feels comfortable now. Good not to have sore points that really needed attention."

As he dressed and checked his phone he had a feeling of satisfaction. He was glad they talked of allowing enough time to heal, and how this massage came at the perfect time for him to assess his body's power to correct past indulgencies given proper care and rest.

He went to the front desk, paid the $80.00 fee, and gave her a $15.00 tip.

"Thank you," he said. "I'll get back with you."

"All right. Don't let it be so long next time. And thank you."

He grabbed the bottle of water set on top of the desk for him, grabbed a few mints from a bowl, and walked out the front door.

Larry was born in 1953 to Doug and Martha Fleming. Larry was a healthy 8.5lbs at birth. He was loved and nurtured from the start as he was Martha's first born. Her three sisters and one brother showed much love to Larry, and support for the new family, especially Tina, the oldest sister. Tina was firm and sure, and guided many aspects of diaper changes and wash, bedding, clothing, and general holding, feeding, and singing to the handsome baby boy. Even their friends and neighbors seemed drawn to this child in a special way helping where needed, someone always coming over to their small apartment on Sunrise Street, a mile away from her parent's house.

Martha met Doug after they graduated from high school. She started college at Spelman, and he worked for Cooper's Drug Store down the street. She and a girlfriend stopped by one afternoon to get a Freezy and Doug made it up for them. He took a liking to Martha right away as she seemed a bit shy and reserved. They all talked while Doug worked to sweep up and move stuff around, and Martha couldn't keep her eyes away from his movements. She liked how funny he could be, and how he seemed to have a special smile for her on the days she came to the store.

He asked her out for a movie at Bailey's Theater and paid the fifteen cents for her ticket. After a while she became pregnant, left school, and took a job at the Needham factory. They married, rented the apartment on Sunrise, and lived there through the birth of their second son, Leroy. Doug started gambling and winning a lot of money at cards and the numbers, was arrested twice, and left town by the time Larry turned five, and Leroy was four. Martha moved back in with her family, returned to college, and earned a degree in education. Doug would call occasionally, but they never got back together. She got a job with the school system and moved to her own place when the boys were nine and ten.

*

"No, I don't have anything stronger here. If you need to go out and get something and come back another day that's fine."

"I'm just a little upset. I've spent my whole life doing good things well and now this. Excuse me for the profanity, I'm just really baffled how I was framed. I didn't see it coming. Man, those guys set me up. Money, I guess; I was blinded by the billionaire thing. Didn't need it of course. Billionaire."

Henson returned to his seat and asked for more water.

"Sure," Larry responded.

"So how do we do this, way back or recent history?"

"Recent. Remember, I'm a counselor, not a business guru or doctor," spoken with a wry smile.

"All right counselor," Henson spoke, taking his suit coat off, "here we go."

He searched the walls and noticed the certified addiction counselor documents, and several articles that said this guy knew his craft. Still, he wasn't sure if he wanted to go through with this conversation.

"Let's start here: In 1997 I pulled off the deal of a lifetime. I'd made some moves, but this was almost too good to be true. I'm a numbers guy, right, and a friend of a friend needed some tax help for his growing electronics business. He had developed a semiconductor that was revolutionary, and was making money hand over fist, as the saying goes. I don't know, well I guess I can tell you the details now, let's just say he personally earned $200,000,000.00 in 1996. He had missed a patent deadline, resolved that, but the whole process of running the company, blah, blah, blah had burned him out and he was ready to sell. I put together a package, bought it, patents, plans, customers, etc. for $120,000,000.00."

Henson starts to laugh to himself, then says with bravado, "I didn't have to pull a weapon!" He laughs uncontrollably for a few seconds, then composes himself.

"As is my custom, I worked very hard for eleven years and grew the business and have shared a lot of profit with the people who have been with me and worked just as hard. All very rich now as well," he says very calmly.

"It all sounds pretty wonderful so far," Larry remarks.

"Well, it took turn for the worse."

When Thomas and Bruce retired from Hobe in June 2008 they talked of the work they'd done there, and how rewarding it had been. The technological equipment they played with was truly amazing, though certain aspects of the research into behavior and intentionality felt wrong. They had given the company their best efforts and were proud of what they accomplished. Thomas was especially proud that he had not mentioned Weapons Eye Sync to anyone. He felt comfortable enough with Bruce's level of expertise and moral fiber to broach the idea of becoming his partner in business, and further develop his idea. Thomas invited Bruce to come to his house on September 30 to discuss an idea he'd been kicking around a few years. Bruce agreed and arrived about 7:15pm.

"Come in."

Bruce comfortably crossed the front threshold.

"Good evening. Nice evening; still warm."

"Yes, come on in; we'll go to the den. Drink?"

"No, I'm fine, thanks."

"Bruce how are you this evening?" Shirley asks as she comes to give him a hug. "Good to see you: how's Mary?"

"Good, she's good. She says hello."

"When are we all going to get together for dinner and a movie?"

"Soon, let's do it soon."

"Tell her to call me and we'll make some plans."

"I'll do it."

Bruce smiles to her as he moves on to the den through the kitchen. Thomas follows him and closed the door behind them.

"Wow can't believe it's been four months!" Thomas starts.

"Yeah, we had a good trip to Arizona. Very relaxing. Sedona, the Canyon; just all over was nice."

"Three weeks?" Thomas asks, yet really confirming what he already knew.

"Right, yeah, great."

"Well," Thomas pauses, "I asked you over to discuss a business proposal. Something you know a lot about and like what we worked on at Hobe. It's something I developed after leaving the police force back in '88. It has to do with weapon recognition, and a perpetrator's abilities to harm law enforcement personnel."

"Sounds exciting."

"Well it is, with a potential to help the good guys, and make us a lot of money. I need you because of your performance control work, how you've uncovered flaws in otherwise foolproof systems. I don't want to discuss too much tonight, and we can go over particulars at another time."

"Yeah, I'm open."

"Good. Tomorrow too soon?"

"Not at all. Early is good."
"8a?"
"Sure. Here?"
"Yeah. 8a. See you in the morning."
"Okay!"
Bruce says goodnight to Shirley and almost floats out the door.

###

Jack Moran was the lead person for the special weapons division of Hobe Phone Company, the government's research arm into behavior and intentionality. Its purpose was to study 'How Our Brothers Evolved,' an ongoing thesis concerned with the peculiar connections between American blacks and whites. They had spent years with the whole White versus Caucasian models, but now the quest had been to resolve the notion that black people from south of the Sahara in Africa, years later, required different systems to penetrate a variance in moral structure. Skin color was the main driver of the studies, but the realities of Caucasians from North Africa, Somalia, or Arabs and some people from India confused the narrow boundaries so far. When Thomas Robinson was recruited in 1986 he had already solved certain issues of physical integrity using sound wave variance, but what he was charged with now to develop was a little scary.

Thomas hired 20 actors for today's skin color recognition tests that Jack had ordered. They ranged from pale white to deep black. He was convinced their sensors could not only detect motives by skin color, but also degrees of intent of a possible crime suspect. Using historical data, he was curious about whether weight and spatial filters could influence translation algorithms. He knew that defined variance could be put into mathematical formulae, but would the device accept changes in brain/body signals?

There were two teams of ten each who were assigned various roles, white normal to dark skin normal, with cultural nuance factored in, i.e., levels of industry, perception of freedom, achievements, expectations, and heritage. These were mixed with propensity for criminal behaviors, and how they were defined by each sub-group. Other indicators were capacity for learning, meaning comprehension, and knowledge of performance parameters. IQ and morality would be assigned and codified later.

The control group would define how the device functioned with basic, old-school intentions. With the test group could it adapt to mixed use motives? The results would show how certain skin color groups define work for hire as a sociological requisite, drug dealing, or identity fraud, for instance. Could the scanning sensor discern accepted procedure, and identify intent, skill level, and the type weapon carried by the individual, all in .82 seconds? This was the stated goal of these tests.

Darlene Jackson enjoyed a good corporate career with the airlines. She worked in HR as an executive trainer and was well regarded in her tight network. She was tall and healthy, working out twice a week, casually dating other professionals, and collected black themed art. She had a master's in social work, and always received excellent yearly reviews for her work performance. She was making $94,000.00 a year when she met Larry. She owned a split-level home in Stone Mountain's West Street community and drove a standard sedan. At 43 years old, she would still be called cute, and had a good, positive circle of girlfriends who met regularly for dinner. All of them were still single, or divorced, so the conversation usually covered four topics: men, finance, travels, and social commentary. Tonight's conversation was about good black men who'd served prison time, and about their age, and whether they should consider dating any?

"What about your brother?" Paula asked Joyce Taylor as Darlene listened intently.

"You know, Ronnie was so good growing up; decent, smart, athletic, family oriented. It was a mild shock when he got busted," Joyce shared.

"What do you mean 'mild'?" Darlene asked.

"Bank Fraud. He covered up so well. He wasn't flashy. We thought he was following suit, working hard, taking classes, getting coached. We just thought all that was paying off well for him."

"What happened?" Darlene followed up, noticing Joyce tense up and withdraw a bit.

"All he said was he was helping some dancers at Johnny's club buy their first homes," Joyce responded.

"How much time?" Paula asked.

"96 months."

"Federal?"

"Yes," Joyce answered.

"When does he get out?" Paula further probes.

"Two months. He's in a half-way house now," Joyce gives them.

"Have y'all gone to see him there?"

"Sure. You want to see him?" Joyce asked Paula.

They all gave a laugh.

"Darlene, didn't you date him one time?" Paula asked.

"Don't even start there!" Darlene shot back.

They all laugh again.

These were five good, fine, black ladies who had lived right, gone to school, and had positive social and family lives. Now, starting middle age, they were honestly searching for the other pieces of their lives.

*

Darlene was introduced to Larry by a mutual friend. They talked a few times by phone and made plans for dinner and to attend a Philosophy Society Lecture afterwards if all was going well. They agreed to meet at a small restaurant near Grady Park at 6 on Saturday September 24, 1998. The lecture was only two miles away.

She arrived first and parked near the front entrance. Larry arrived and parked a few spaces away, closer to the street. They greeted each other warmly and went in.

"Thanks for coming," spoke David, the chef owner who greeted them.

"We're glad to be here," spoke Larry. "Rich told me to tell you hello."

"Richie Cooper?" questioned David.

"Yeah. Good friend."

"Yes, he is. How's his wife, Christine?" asked David.

"Good. Good. Her surgery went well."

"Such good people," David shared.

"How about over here, window view of the park?"

"Looks great," Darlene spoke up as she looked towards Larry.

"Sure, looks good to me," Larry offered.

David gestured to the adequately sized table for two, assisted Darlene with her chair and nodded to Larry.

"Thanks," Larry and Darlene said in unison.

"Justin will be your waiter. Oh, here he is now."

Justin steps up to the table, smiles and says, "Hello."

David pauses, "I don't know your names," he says, a bit embarrassed.

"I'm Darlene, he's Larry."

"Thanks," David says, "My bad, okay. I'm going now. Justin will take good care of you."

David walks off quickly.

"Drinks?" Justin asks.

"Water, water," Larry and Darlene answer.

Justin asks, as he's giving them a menu, "First time here?"

"Yes," they each respond.

"Hopefully, you'll have a good experience. We're quite proud of what we do here."

'We've heard good things," Larry responds.

"Okay, make yourselves comfortable, and I'll return in a few minutes with your waters."

"Thank you," Larry again responds.

Since it was still warm for late September Darlene was tastefully dressed in a light sweater. Larry was casual with khaki slacks, open collar dress shirt and a suit coat.

"This seems nice," Darlene observes.

"Yeah," Larry asserts.

They each fumble nervously while reading the menus.

"Well here we are," Darlene starts.

"Shrimp, scallops okay?" Larry asks.

"Sure," she answers.

"Thanks again for agreeing to this."

"Sure. I needed to get out."

"Why is that?" he asks.

"Work's been busy lately with 20 new hires, and I've had to train them all in phase one; introductions, rules, ethics, SOPs, all that before they get to their workstations."

"Sounds hectic?"

"Just busy; four hours of that each day then my other work. But I enjoy it. I want to prepare them for our work culture, and I want to be as thorough as possible."

"I'm sure."

"Well I think you have to give people your best. This is where they form notions about what's to come and what's expected of them, as well as what we give. I want them to know why we're successful, and what they'll need to do to add to the growth of the company. Of course, we've screened them, checked their resumes, accomplishments, other histories, drug tests, criminal background checks, etc. We're not social services."

"Wow, I probably couldn't get a job there," Larry says, jokingly.

"Naaahhh, you're fine; I know who you are."

"Oh, you checked me out?" he asks.

"Somewhat. You'll have to fill in a few gaps," she laughs. "How about me, what do you know?"

"Vanilla, or rather chocolate chip. What you see is what you get."

"That's kind of you."

They laugh a bit longer, and shyly eye each other for a few seconds.

"Here we go. I brought some lemon slices just in case you'd want to add them to your water," Justin announces.

"How thoughtful," Darlene says.

"How would y'all like to start," he asks, setting their waters on paper coasters, and placing the lemon wedges in the center of the table on a small glass dish.

"Shrimp, scallops, a crab cake we can split," Larry orders, looking directly at Darlene.

She nods okay.

"Sure. I'll get that right out. Questions about dinner choices?"

"Not yet. Thanks," they answer.

Darlene thinks Larry is a good-looking man. "So far, he seems okay," she thinks, as she studies his actions.

FIRST

Rita seemed glad to see Larry this afternoon. He was walking fast and didn't have time to spare. It was five thirty and his group started at six.

She was fully dressed in a coat and a woolen cap on her head. She was rocking back and forth, sitting on the bench, a fast-food bag to her left, crumpled as if the food had been eaten, and the wrapping paper, or an empty carton was inside. Larry knew he had to make time for her, so he walked towards her.

"Counselor," she almost shouted to him.

"Hey Rita," he greeted her.

"Your granddaddy lived near here too, over on Irwin Street. Your grandmamma and two kids. He was a great man too. Wise. Wise. You are great, you know? Tell them about the new dream."

"Rita, I've got to..."

"6 o'clock. I know. But don't be afraid, old man dream needs to rest. New dream. Tell them about the new dream."

"Thank you, Rita."

She smiles, away from him as he walks off to the office.

###

Four people were standing outside Larry's office door when he stepped off the elevator. He smiled, slowed his pace, and greeted them.

"Hey y'all. Let me get to the door here."

He puts his key into the cylinder, turns to open it and steps inside. He turns on the overhead lights, walks over to a lamp on the main table, turns it on, turns around and says, as his clients start in, "Come over here, I'll get you signed in."

He sits at the table, pulls a sign in sheet from a folder, retrieves a pen and a receipt book from the drawer, and starts taking the $60.00 fee from each one: "Name, probation officer, 1st or 2nd DUI, or other offense," he questions, as he takes the money, writes down their name and other information, stacks the money in a pile in front of him, makes change if necessary, or says he'll give it to them later. They line up, and one by one he signs them in as seven others show up before six.

"Have a seat in the group room," he announces, "We'll start in a few minutes. I'll pass out receipts at the end of group."

They all take seats, talk amongst themselves, and wait for Larry to come back.

The group room, like the reception area, had beautiful watercolor pictures on the walls. Two were fall scenes, two were beach scenes, and one was like an outdoor snapshot from New Mexico, hills, and a valley near the Rio Grande somewhere. The chairs are high back-office types on casters, and you could move around or stay set in one place.

"Okay, let's get started," Larry announces. "My name is Larry Fleming, Certified Addiction Counselor, and I'm glad to see everybody,

ADDICTION AND THE NEW DREAM

but I'm sure most of you are not happy to be here. I try to teach and entertain, and I hope you'll get more out of this than just your letter of completion. That depends on you. The rules are simple; listen, talk, respect each other, get honest, and grow up a little bit. I'm a counselor, not your probation officer. The legal stuff is on you, whether you did it or not that's for you and the courts. What we talk about here is addiction, alcoholism, or bullshit; you lie to me, I'll lie to you. I'm a dope fiend. I was out there for eighteen years if you've done it I probably did it too. One difference is I've been clean and sober 28 years now and have a pretty good life. It's what you want to do about your problem. How it works is I'll probably talk the first hour, you talk the second hour, and then we'll all talk the third hour. Sometimes we'll watch an educational video, sometimes a movie. This is not 'AA,' or any other 'A,' people who go there want to be there, you've been forced to come, and pay; those are free services. But, if you are an addict, or alcoholic, or just pretending, you already know. I've been at this a long time and some of what you are going to say I'll think it's crazy, and some of what I say you'll think it's crazy. Hopefully, at the end of three hours we've all learned something about ourselves, or someone else."

All fidget a little, adjust their seated positions, and take a breath.

"Now, I generally don't like profanity, but I will go 'ghetto' if I have to. We're not going to argue too long about anything. I will call the police, quick, if a real threat is made. Like I said, respect, civility, and we will have classes on those topics." Larry takes a deep breath. "Okay, let's do the question-and-answer thing. First, let's go around the room and introduce ourselves. We'll start to my left and go around the room. State your name, and why you're here. All right let's start here," he gestures to his left.

"My name is Lester Ross, 2nd DUI."

"My name is Sharon Fuller, drug possession."

"My name is Robert Thompson, theft by taking."

"I'm Johnny, I'm just here man," he says, as the group laughs.

"I'm Tori Davis, solicitation."
"My name is Doris Jones, DUI."
"I'm Sarah, pot."
"I'm Joan, heroin addict, theft."
"Davis, public indecency, pot."
"Mr. James Harris, alcohol consumption."
"Gina Rawlings, gave cop a blow job."
The group bursts out in laughter for a few seconds.

From the individual evaluations sent over to him, and the couple that he had done, the average age of the group was 24, seven were high school graduates, two dropped out, and one had a GED. Doris Jones was a professor in African American Literature. None of these clients had done hard prison time, although three had served nine months in County. Most had been arrested, sent to probation, and the courts had ordered substance abuse counseling. Larry knew this population well and looked forward to each group session.

After group, walking up to the bus stop, Larry thought of his nine-month tour of duty with the 4th Infantry Division in West Germany in 1973. He remembered thinking he not only let his Uncle Lewis down, who soldiered on German soil during WWII, but Generals Frank O. Davis, Jr. and Sr., men who distinguished themselves there as well, in the air and on the land. Men who beat segregation by their performance, beat it by determination, sacrifice, and a will to excel. Jr., who led the Tuskegee Airmen to unparalleled success with their escort missions, meeting several German FW-190s and ME 262 jet aircraft, destroying several, and damaging others, showed that black men too had the good stuff, dignity, precision, and reserve. Larry thought how they would not have approved of how he relieved himself of any moral fortitude, had resigned any mental agility, had become, by his abuse of drugs, a low life, unworthy of any mention of having once been a military man, though to his credit he did perform several top-secret missions that were successful; two sanctioned, one not.

It took three months for Thomas and Bruce to get the business structure in place. They had to hire a law firm, accountants, a sales force, consultants for trade laws governing foreign commerce, and general office staff. They found out about the Mears building in downtown Atlanta and leased about 10,000 square feet for three years. There had been much discussion about the location, and they decided here their clients would get a good view of the city driving in from Hartsfield-Jackson, or an outlying smaller airport. They figured, rightly, that most of the buyers they were after would come by private jet anyway, and have limousines bring them to the office from there.

Of course, Thomas Robinson, owner, was designated CEO, and Bruce Walker was given 20% of the company, and named COO. By December 2008 they were fully operational.

*

The people who had been following Mr. Henson now followed Larry Fleming. They couldn't understand why Mr. Henson came to Mr. Fleming's office each Tuesday at 2pm. They knew Fleming was a substance abuse counselor of some distinction, but Henson had no known addiction issues. Today, warm, and sunny, Larry was out for an early morning jog through his neighborhood and the two spies knew their cover had been blown, that his pattern was different, and that he took a call for the first time in 20 runs over the past two months. It was Wallace Henson.

"Hey Wallace, how are you?"

"Fine, look, can we move our session to noon today?"

"Sure. See you then."

"Okay, thanks."

Wallace hung up and turned to the young woman next to him.

"Okay, that's done. What's next?" he asks her.

Sally Penfield was a Mergers and Acquisitions specialist with White, Farmer, and White. They were helping Henson with the purchase of Weapons Eye Sync, and some patent issues.

"So, will I own them or not, and can we buy the company?" he asks her.

"You will own them. Mr. Robinson had done some work for Hobe Phone Company and they're maintaining he stole some of their technology. He says he'd already developed that type sensor and had a patent for it. In his work for them they wanted a modified version of a chip for not only the skin color detection capability, but also the IQ component. That's what he and Mr. Walker created for them. Robinson's earlier chip was primarily about intent of action. Robinson and Walker have always said when they left Hobe they left that work there because it was work for hire. Mr. Robinson had produced sketches, dates, patent numbers, and certified copies of his invention. Plus, Blintel Corporation was way ahead of them both in those departments. Their stuff goes back to the 70s. We have a court date January 19, 2012. Thomas and Bruce have signed depositions and will not have to appear for us, or the other side; they've been ruled neutral."

"That's not good; we need them for our case, don't we?"

"The phone company wants the patents, not your money."

Henson laughs slightly.

The Supreme Court sided with Weapons Eye Sync, stating that the Federal Appeals Court wrongly overturned the lower court's ruling about the three patents. Weapons Eye Sync keeps its exclusive rights to the chip, and thus can go forward with a sale of the company.

SECOND

Mary and Shirley rode down to the office on Thursday to touch up the place. Most of the furnishings were in place, pictures hung, and art pieces set well on their stands. There was a good mix of wood, metal, and glass. Chairs were ergonomic, but not exotic, the ten-foot high ceilings gave the place an airy comfort. The modest sized individual offices were staged to welcome PCs, laptops, flip phones, and recreational listening devices. General staff was a good mix of military, law enforcement, educators, experienced administrative staff, and top sales professionals. The research department had physicists, psychologists, medical doctors, and a nurse; sometimes they outsourced testing, yet Bruce was highly skilled in design and quality control, so he would oversee any difficulties with the products they devised. He was hands on, but not intrusive.

Bruce and Thomas met the wives when they entered, standing at attention like two schoolboys who had won the science fair.

"Ladies, entrez-vous, sil vous plait," Bruce spoke up.

"Merci," both ladies responded as all chuckled.

"Come to preview the finished product?" Thomas followed, "Let's have a tour."

The ladies entered, professionally dressed in neat skirts, and well-fitting jackets over white blouses. They wore low heeled black shoes. Shirley was a striking blonde whose air of culture and refinement was in abeyance in this setting. She didn't need to prance around the work force. Mary, being more modest by nature, as well as Bruce, didn't have any airs to 'put on,' she was moderate with a warm smile. They'd all had enough years together in work and social settings to understand the strengths and vulnerabilities of each other. Both families were comfortable financially with the assurance that more big money was on the way. Plus, they all felt measured by their actions and not the money.

"Let's start in my office," Thomas presented, "Then we'll walk the track."

Track being the reference for the flow of the office's design, almost like an automobile assembly line, one part connects to the other part, start to finish.

*

History:

Wallace Henson, 63, male, CPA, intact family, two brothers, younger.

1970 Graduates Lakeside High School

1971-1973 US Army

1974 Married Sally Rogers. They have four children two girls, and two boys.

1977 Graduates University of Georgia; CPA 1979

1979-1989 Works for the IRS

1989 Opens CPA business with two employees: grosses $160,000.00

1991 Bought, then sold three investment properties (houses). Earned $30,000.00

1993 Bought, then sold eight investment properties (houses). Earned $110,000.00

1995 Bought receivables worth $800,000.00, repackaged, then sold for $600,000.00. Earned $200,000.00

1997 Bought Semi-Conductor Company with 32 employees.

1998 Incorporated Henson Technologies.

2011 Offers to buy Weapons Eye Sync

2012 Completes deal for WES

Wallace Henson 5/2012

"Like most of the people I know, I've worked hard and had good results. I've been blessed with good health, and at sixty-three I feel pretty good. I guess since the divorce I've not done well in relationships," Wallace was saying.

"Why do you think that's so?" Larry asks him.

"Well, if I'm honest, it could have something to do with my drinking. I can get mean towards women when I drink. Just a lot I didn't get to practice. I turned to business, and 'business relationships,' and I don't think I have a clue what it really means to be intimate with a woman."

"Anything steady now?"

"About four years ago. She was nice, and we did all the nice stuff, travel, movies, art stuff, dinners; you know."

"Had she moved in?"

"No. I'd sleep at her place, she at mine, but it lacked something."

"Any other kinds of relationships?" Larry asks without being direct.

"No, straight. No problems there. Like a friend says, I have trouble 'committing' to the relationship."

"Probably the booze. Let's see," Larry reaches behind him for Wallace's file, then reads softly, "15, starts drinking, tried pot, didn't like it, sniff or two of cocaine in college, modest drinking after college, out of control for a few months in '99, quit for two years, up and down since. Two steady relationships, one two years, one five. They broke off—, no ring. Heavy the last five months, suicidal. Suicidal?"

"Let's talk about that," Wallace jumps in.

"Take your time, this is big stuff. Where are you right now with that?" Larry asks cautiously.

"Nothing now. I wrote it down because when I got out of control sometimes, I'd really feel disgusted. Never a plan."

"Last drink?"

"Yesterday."

"Are you taking any medications?"

"Something for sleep sometimes."

"From a Doc?"

"OTC."

"How often?"

"Once, twice a week at times."

"What else?"

"That's it."

"Any drugs of abuse now, crack, meth, heroin on the weekends?" Larry smiles as he's asking.

"Not my style."

"How about some of your, umm, dates, girlfriends in the past?"

"Not even. They've been mostly the 'wine with dinner' types who otherwise don't drink, and don't finish those when ordered."

"So, are you a drunk?" Larry asks directly.

"Maybe. But what's going on now is the stress of buying this company. There are some social implications that are disturbing."

"How so?"

"Man, we don't have but a few minutes left; that answer is long."

"Okay, let's wrap up for today. Now tell me..."

Wallace interrupts.

"I used to hunt and target shoot, and I have two 'nines, an old school .38 for effect, and a rifle. If you say it, I'll give them to you, or Nelson, or whoever. If some clown tries to rob me so be it!"

"Your call."

"I'll keep them for now."

"The drinking?"

"I may need help with that."

"AA?"

"Twice. Not for me."

"How sick do you get when you try to stop. Vomiting, shakes, heart palpitations, sweats?"

"Some weakness and restlessness; no vomiting, no palpitations, some shakiness."

"High blood pressure?"

"It goes up. If I drink a lot of water and orange juice and eat something I'm usually all right."

"Call me tomorrow near noon whether you drink tonight or not."

"I won't drink, I'll have my friend come by and check on me. She's a trained nurse. I don't need a paper trail before closing this deal."

"What's most important?"

"I get that. I'll call tomorrow, and if you think we need to do something else I'll trust your decision."

"Does your friend know addiction medicine?"

"Psych nurse, Ledford a few years ago. She'll check my vitals. I'll give her your number. I don't want to die, and I do know I need help."

"Okay."

"How do you know all this? Nelson didn't say much except you're experienced?"

"Big problem back in the day. We'll talk more about me later. Stay safe, stay around."

"You're a comedian too?"

"Send in the clowns."

"Don't bother, they're here."

They have a good laugh, Wallace stands, looks Larry in the eyes and says, "Thanks."

###

Matthew Howard, MD, head of training for WES, wanted the R&D unit to hire a few minority temporary workers. He specified two African Americans, a Hispanic, and a Middle Easterner. Also, he mentioned that it would be helpful if they were recruited from a half-way house connected to federal inmates from prison. Plus, that they were at least 42 years old, and had been in prison since they were at least 24 years old, particularly crack dealers, as they would make the best subjects for study with the next phase of trials on the M2635 unit, intent versus motive.

*

Both Thomas and Shirley knew about secrets, she was thinking after the lecture. She had dated a black guy in college. He was nice and civil, and liked art and literature, and the race component gave the relationship a nice edge, but she was high octane, and he just didn't have the 'juice' to get her home, so to speak. Thomas was different, he was cordial, bright, and a liar. When they started dating he was already successful in his work, but when talking about his family he'd fudge a bit. It was only after a few more dates that he told her about Ron, his mentally challenged younger brother. He was not ashamed about the fact but was uncomfortable talking about it. She was not sure if she should ever mention Randall based on some comments Thomas made when they were out for a movie one Sunday afternoon.

"Probably a crack dealer," Thomas had commented, "What's a young black boy doing in a car like that!? I'm sure he's not a doctor."

"He could be," Shirley answered.

"No way. That one has not done a day of legal work in his life. Look how he's driving, parking like he owns the place. And I bet that white girl with him is a prostitute."

"Thomas, you're kidding. It's 1983. You're kidding, right?"

"I'm telling you, dope dealer. He'll be in jail in a few months."

"Thomas, come on?"

"All right, none of my business," he says, holding his hands up in the air.

"Well, with some dreams and myths, religious notions help us to know, and I quote here, "Dream is real." In other words, your real self will be revealed to you based on choices. Thank You."

Much applause. The hostess comes up and shakes Dr. Yates' hand, turns sideways, gestures to him, and the gathered applaud louder.

"We want to thank Dr. Yates for another stirring lecture."

The doctor takes a bow and walks to his seat on the front row.

"Wow, another good one," she says. We'd like to thank you all for coming tonight. Our next lecture is November 13, and Dr. Vincent Brown will discuss, 'What If I Knew?' his most recent thesis on Mung's personal unconsciousness. Goodnight everyone. Be sure to join us."

Shirley and Thomas were enjoying these small lectures at Freda Johnson's home. Twelve was about the right number of people for food and these kinds of intellectual classes. They both were readers and were well versed in this lecture series, and it made for a good date night as they seemed to be getting more serious about becoming a couple.

THIRD

Larry picked up the paper again and felt the anger, 'Forget American Blacks?' He'd kept it in a file folder under some clothes in the gym bag he's had since getting sober. He drifted in thought, away from the anger, to how he felt competing against the New York basketball players when he was in basic training in Missouri back in '72. He'd always heard the best 'ball' players came from there, and here he was, from Atlanta, Georgia, head and shoulders with these guys, dribbling, shooting, passing, play making the way he had against Blue and the boys back home. It was second nature to him just like the drills and marches, handling his pack, or helping Davis, the white kid from South Georgia who couldn't keep up sometimes, and how he thanked Larry for his support. Or the way he handled himself when the white drill sergeant from Ohio said in a class one time, "Make that brass shiny as a black man's ass;" somehow the sergeant had overlooked the only black soldier in the room, or perhaps he didn't care. In any event Larry went up to him after class and got a private apology, instead of making a big deal out of it.

*

Whatever the redacted parts of the paper were about he would like to recover them. Larry and the boys had survived different kinds of hell, here, and in Vietnam, back in the day, and they had come home to good jobs with the airlines, or the car companies; some to the Post Office, or airplane builders. Now, so many years later, it was when he ran into one of his grow up playmates, like Ralph Palmer, who still had that quiet calm and sense of fellowship they portrayed when playing for the Simpson Street Rams football team 50 years ago, showing then skills to master the game. His trials as a black heroin addict, compared to the challenges of combat in Southeast Asia, though different, yet the street gun fights of those Friday nights in Wedgewood qualified him as a combat participant. Sure, a different kind of combat, different hand to hand, different strategies, motives, and yet, the same need to play the cards as dealt, the same intent, oddly, to be a good man trying to do good things, and continually having it corrupted by the necessities of getting along, leading the 'men' on a mission to save the high school's honor, thinking of a simple fight when the troops had guns, and then getting kicked out of school because he was recognized as the football star, Larry Fleming; the others merely anonymous bad actors cheating a moral cause. And yet, now, talking to Palmer, both standing tall, mature, good men still, not bitter, or angry, older black men still ready to serve, still leading by example.

*

"Sometimes it's just hard to talk to black folk. The ones of us who stayed good, went to school, fought off the bad influences, and graduated school can't relate on certain levels. Or we didn't get the slave mentality, or the 40 acres and a mule thing, we just got up each day and went about it. My mother and father didn't have a master's degree, but they showed me the work ethic/payoff route. You know mama dropped out of college to have my sister, and daddy never went, but they just kept on," Darlene was saying as they rode the scenic roads from Santa Fe headed to Taos. "And, it was not pretense, just like it's not now. Certain kids I couldn't relate to, and that was black or white. Now, like your buddy, Roderick, he's a fool. I know you love him like your brother, and his wife and kids are precious, and at work, no comparison. But that boy is a fool, the language he uses sometimes, so out of date the way he describes certain women, and people in general. I just can't stand to be around him. And I know he's not going to change. And y'all get together for the Super Bowl, and I know you got it this time, so I just get ready. It's okay."

"Thank you. I know, it's crazy. And you know he's all about black folks, but his language..."

"David and your other friends cleaned up their acts, why can't he?" she adds.

ADDICTION AND THE NEW DREAM 33

"Look, there's El Chimayo. "

"Good, I got to pee."

They spent about an hour on the church grounds soaking up the October light, the fresh air, and the feeling that a force was at work to protect them if they maintained a spiritual balance. They were not church people back home, but still felt the presence of their ancestors, here.

*

Premium Photo, the subsidiary for research at Weapons Eye Sync was in the final testing phase for its most up to date device, the 1027BH. It not only could identify weapons, but gave vital signs, and could separate intent from motive in .79 seconds. The skin color issue was still troublesome, and that's why today's series of tests were so important.

"I still can't believe there's such a big difference in moral valuation," Dr. Timothy Lowe was sharing with Dr. Howard. "We've trained them, the feds 'trained' them, what else?"

"Tim, they're just different, and you can't change that. Nature/nurture, Science 101 remember?"

"Look, how many white people do you see looting a store during a riot? Asian, Islamic, European, South American? You see what I'm saying? And what does the data show, starting about 1958, American Blacks are just different, and if you don't factor that in we'll never get the edge," Dr. Howard continued.

"Is that still that slavery stuff you guys down here like to hold on to?" Doctor Lowe questions.

"They do, and that's 60% of the issue."

"How about mixed race, slave owner's kids?"

"See, that's why we can't have this discussion. They too are different," Dr. Howard maintains.

"And what about their kids on down the line?" Tim asks.

"See, this is where Southern man messed it up for all of us, they're still white."

"Okay, I get that; bring in the criminals."

"One by one?" Dr. Howard asks.

"Yes, Dr. Lowe responds."

Unannounced, Thomas Robinson was in the parking lot about to come in. He was on his phone to Bruce who had mentioned today's testing and invited the boss. About the time Dr. Howard opened the door to the holding area Mr. Robinson was pushing it open. Thomas spoke to the temps there and had a quizzed look on his face.

"Dr." he spoke.

"Mr. Robinson, glad you could join us," adjusting quickly. "Is Mr. Walker coming as well?"

"Yes, he's about five minutes away."

"Good. We were about to begin. It will take about that much time to get set."

"Mr. Robinson, good to see you again," spoke Dr. Lowe as he walks over to him.

"Dr. Lowe, my pleasure."

Dr. Lowe continues past Thomas to summon the first person to come into the lab.

Dr. Howard was a bit surprised by that action, as he'd offered to bring them in.

"Mr. Casey, Orlando Casey."

A tall, fair skinned man stands, smiles, and walks toward the doctor. "Doctor," he says immediately.

"Yes," Doctor Lowe answers nervously. "Come on in.

*

Orlando Casey, 43, 6'1", 210lbs, drug dealer from Detroit. High blood pressure, no other health issues, served 13 years locked up, eight in the penitentiary, five in the camp, has been at the halfway house three months. Crack and marijuana, 121 IQ. Midrange dealer, possible murder suspect, not proven. 10 kids by four women. High school education, business courses at Georgia Perimeter, still controls a real estate business. Has $800,000.00 cash being held by relatives. Cooperative.

"Mr. Casey, thanks for coming. Are they keeping you busy in the warehouse?"

"Yes sir, four hours a day."

"I'm Dr. Tim Lowe, this is Dr. Howard, and that's Mr. Thomas Robinson," he gestures all around. "Dr. Joyce Taylor will join us shortly. Have a seat."

They all sit in chairs arranged in a circle, with two empties for Joyce and Bruce. Dr. Lowe continues to review the file on Mr. Casey. Then he begins.

"Mr. Casey, have you had a chance to read over the handout?"

"Yes sir."

"Do you have any questions?"

"Not now. Sounds interesting."

"I have a couple to ask you before we begin the testing."

"That's fine."

They all adjust their seated positions, with Mr. Robinson crossing his legs tightly, Dr. Howard shifting as if he has some back issues, Mr. Casey sitting straight up, and Tim getting more comfortable with the clipboard in his hand, dropping his pen once, smiling nervously, looking around, then begins his questions.

"May I call you Orlando?" he asks.

"Yeah." Answered in a friendly way.

"Okay, is your mother white, and your father black?"

"Actually, she's what you call mixed. Her daddy was white, and her mother was black."

"And you agree to participate in the line of testing as outlined on the form we gave you?"

"Yeah, it's all right."

"Okay, there will be a series of scenarios presented, and you'll act naturally. You don't have to be right, just right on!"

The group laughs at this attempt at humor. A gentle knock is heard on the door to the lab and Bruce and Joyce enter.

"Hello everyone," Dr. Taylor speaks.

"Gentlemen," Mr. Walker says, and walks to Mr. Casey, who is standing, introduces himself and Dr. Taylor. Drs. Lowe and Howard, and Mr. Robinson, who are standing as well, shake hands with the new arrivals, then they all sit.

"Well, Mr. Casey, thanks for participating in our study," Dr. Taylor says, as she retrieves a pen from her padded folder.

"You're welcome ma'am," Orlando answers.

There was an awkward tension in the room as they all sat silently for a few seconds. Even though Tim was the head researcher, this segment was based on data provided by Dr. Taylor.

"Dr. Taylor." Dr. Lowe announces for her to begin.

"Excuse me," the boss speaks up. "Mr. Casey, could you give us a few moments. Why don't you go back to the warehouse, and we'll call you when we're ready?"

"Sure, no problem. I still get paid, right? I finished my shift there for the day, and I have to return to the half-way house in two hours, and I can't be late."

"We'll get you back on time, and you get paid for the extra time," Thomas says.

Orlando gets up, nods to the group, and walks out the door, almost slamming it.

After a moment Bruce asks, "What's up chief?"

"Are you kidding me, or was this to be a fail test?"

"How do you mean?" Dr. Lowe asks, as well as Dr. Taylor.

"That guy's almost white, and I was feeling like he had taken over the room. Can you test for that?"

"Well, actually this was to be a 'cold' test. 1027BH should catch all that," Dr. Howard spoke up.

"And Dr. Taylor, you're sure about his lineage?" Mr. Robinson asks, showing some concern about her proficiency. I thought you were going to start the final testing on darker skin subjects and mix the rest of the schema?" Thomas asks.

"We could have, but everything to this point has checked out," she says.

"Bruce?" he looks to his partner.

"I trust the test design elements. Of course, what we must know is how sophisticated it really is, the ORT chip I mean. Can it filter for what you're asking in what, .79 second time frame? That we'll find out soon," Bruce says. "I trust Dr. Taylor's nuanced approach."

"Okay. Have the gentleman return, and I'll watch," Thomas offers.

Dr. Howard nods to Dr. Taylor with a wry smile on his face.

*

"What up?" Orlando asks as he re-enters the lab.

"Excuse us?" Dr. Taylor responds.

"Did you go smoke something when you went out?" asks Dr. Lowe.

"Well I went and hit a little something, you know. Y'all didn't have it together so I thought it might be better for the test. It's all about the test, right?" he says.

"You may be on to something?" Thomas speaks up. "Let's you and I act out the first scenario; step over here."

Mr. Robinson guides him to a table on a side wall; the others look on in awe.

"All right, here you see a gun, a knife, and a bent hook, eight inches long. I want you to choose one, walk about 20 yards down to the back wall, and face the wall."

Mr. Casey follows direction. Thomas goes over to a cabinet, takes out the flip phone like device with the keyboard and three-inch diameter screen. He touches a button on the side for three seconds, and a light comes on the screen, with a series of symbols and numbers. After a few seconds, the screen clears but stays aglow.

"Now I want you to think like I just cussed your mama out, and called you a fag, and a punk."

Before Thomas could finish the rest of his fake tirade Orlando had turned and was running for him.

"You motherfucker kiss my ass!" he shouted as he got closer.

When Orlando was within 10 yards Thomas clicked the control button on the device, once then twice. Orlando kept coming towards him but stopped short of bumping into Mr. Robinson. Everyone was winded by the rush of energy, and Bruce requested all to sit after a few deep breaths if needed.

"Wow!" exclaimed Dr. Tim.

"You got that right!" seconded Dr. Matthew.

Dr. Taylor stood, with a look on her face that suggested a mother about to say, 'boys, boys cut that out!' Thomas had the widest smile on his face as he viewed the screen.

"Yes, yes, everyone, sit, please," Thomas says.

They all chose the same chairs they had before. After a few seconds Bruce speaks:

"Mr. Casey, thank you. How do you feel?" he asks.

"Good, that was fun. Thank y'all for giving me a chance."

"Do you have enough time to get back to half-way on time?' Bruce asks, genuinely concerned.

"The buses run on time over here, and it's not rush hour. I should be fine."

"How's the warehouse?" Bruce asks, stalling a bit, knowing that his colleagues are dying to get the results, especially the way Thomas is glued to the screen, still smiling.

"Thanks again to y'all. It's great, a great job, and Frank is the best."

"Okay, good. When do you come back?" Dr. Matthew Howard asks.

"Next Friday," he answers.
"Okay, see you then, bye," everyone says.
He gets up quickly and goes on his way.

*

"Man, oh man, oh man," Thomas exclaims and twirls around to show everyone the screen, knowing they couldn't see it clearly, so he begins to read the results.

"Weapon-8-inch hook; intent-murder; motive-high; blood pressure-increased; ability-true; skin type-mixed race; time-.77."

They all clap, laugh, jump up and high five each other, some tear up a bit.

"Gosh damn!" Dr. Lowe shouts.
"Yea, Yea!" Dr. Howard screams.
"Praise the Lord," Dr. Taylor shouts.
"Amen," Mr. Walker adds.
"Great job!" Mr. Robinson affirms.

FOURTH

"It's a lot of good people out there," Darlene was saying to Alice. "Good people doing a lot of good all the time. Too bad the news shows can only give us 3% of it a day."

"Yeah, they'd go out of business if they tried to give us more, '18-year-old black youth cut white lady's yard; didn't try to rob her.' Or, 72-year-old white man didn't have black youth arrested for sagging jeans,' Alice offered.

They both give out a big laugh.

"Why is it so hard to have a decent discussion about race in this country on TV?" Darlene asked, getting up to get more coffee. "Need a hit?" she asked Alice.

"No thanks." Alice gets up and follows her into the kitchen and looks out the back bank of windows to the woods behind the house.

"And it shouldn't be hard, especially down here since we all grew up together one way or another. Slaves, owners, maids, yard men, executives, doctors; since the early 1800s we've been connected," Darlene proposed.

"True, but that color thing just can't be overcome, and no one can be honest about that," Alice offered. "I was in the grocery store the other day and the pretty, young cashier resembled my niece, facial structure, long hair, cute smile, gentle features, body size, and I remember thinking, "But she's not quite as pretty. And I know it was skin color because of some darker spots on her forehead. And I don't know if it's wrong or not? Did she seem just as smart? Yes. Was she courteous, and efficient? Yes. Did she seem mean or angry? No. So, I don't know; but it was curious."

"I don't know. One of my girlfriends asked if I had not met Larry would I have considered dating a white guy. And to me the question has always been, 'Would a white guy consider dating me?' Now why is that I've wondered?" Darlene posits, "And the whole black man, white man thing is terrible anyway. I'll ask you, generally, do white men feel black men are as smart as they are?"

"Okay, we're going there. Generally, no. I think there is some relevance to the whole family dispersal thing, and I think there is a race color hate thing there as well. Seems like some black men are afraid of each other. But I digress. The point I was trying to make is that the whole nurture thing was set back, and I'll guess here, a hundred years in the black community."

"Because of drugs?"

"No, going back. The migration thing in the 30s, and the war years. That's my take: no science," Alice humbly offers.

"You know, I'll go with that. Some of the lessons grandpa had to offer were never passed down. Young men had to grow up without a certain structure that was put in place in the 20s by my granddad, and of course, the other blacks born at the turn of the century. They didn't have the extended formal education, but they had the family and the work ethic. I don't think I could manage my sister coming to live with us, and my grandmother talked all the time about siblings and cousins coming to stay with them at times. I think something has been lost there," Darlene shares. "There are just so many layers to this conversation, it's hard to get people to sit long enough and stay with each other's true thoughts, and histories."

"That's a good point," Alice responds. "We got help from some family during a rough patch in the 50s, but I think what was different we were raised to be independent early, though resources were around. If we were going to eat we still had to learn where to hunt. We were given a weapon, and time in the field together, but the duty was ours after they completed theirs. Or maybe put more simply, we were given 'stuff,' and the black culture didn't have stuff to give, and thus the uneven balance. Most black men didn't have the same means to prove themselves. It was a different kind of jungle."

They both pause, eye each other, hug, and cry for a time.

Shirley and Mary were becoming better friends as their husbands' business flourished. They were out for lunch at the Thai WA Noodle Shop on Grove Avenue in Downtown Roswell. It was a small, upscale restaurant that sat twenty comfortably. The small two-person tables were mixed wrought iron and beveled glass, and the three that sat four were repurposed wood from a closed factory from around the corner, circa 1923. They were given a large table, and were glad that their friend Helen, who lives nearby, may join them. They sat, settled, ordered tea and basil rolls, and looked about the charming courtyard outside their window, to Mary's left. A gray feral cat could be seen scurrying past and running into the furniture repair shop next door, run by Kevin Taylor's family the past 62 years, 'Good Work in Time' the sign on the side of the building read. Seeing this, Mary drifted off in thought to the last time she and Bruce were in Hawaii. She remembered the peace and gratitude she felt for experiencing the 'out there' of that position in the Pacific

Ocean. Her artistic nature was soothed by the almost hands-off approach of the sky, and the sing to me nature of the waters. She relished her love for Bruce and his ability to come home and sit with her, stroke her hair, look her in the eyes and truly ask about her day. It was all so dreamy and ordered by the universe that they could live a life of leisure, and yet, not have to move to a bigger house, or a better neighborhood, only because they had simply worked well and now enjoy a serenity preached by the deacons, those gentle souls of service who show up, and guide the reverend when he falls short, who support the efforts of the choir members, and class room teachers, who shepherd the flock, and pray for all as they are free. Yet, something was disturbing about Bruce that she couldn't quite put a finger on.

"Mary, what would you like?" Shirley asked, not noticing that Mary had gone to a parallel universe where the 'wiggles' of creativity reside.

"Oh wow, thanks, yes, let's see?" she answered still a bit cloudy.

They both look over the menu and order noodle soup with pork. The server brought their tea and rolls about the time Helen arrived. She took a seat, ordered what they were having, and grabbed both of their hands.

"So good to see you both; thanks for coming out this way."

"Absolutely," Shirley offers.

"You look well," Mary says to her.

"You too," she responds. "The rich ladies I always knew you were!"

They all laugh and share toothy grins at the fun of it all.

"How are those boys doing?" Helen asks, looking more towards Shirley.

"Just fine," she answers, looking to Mary who nods in agreement. "And how about Davis, is he still working for the pros?"

"He is, and he's doing great. In and out of town a lot lately; those athletes look good in their uniforms on Sunday, but they're a headache during the week; in trouble all the time, especially those good-looking black ones!"

"Helen!" Shirley responds.

"Of course, not all of them; but enough," she gives. "Every once-in-a-while he has one, with their lawyers, over to the house for a conference. It's all I can do to stay calm! Did I just say that?" as she blushes big time.

They all laugh and give each other semi-high fives.

"Do we need to move on?" Mary says, laughing the hardest.

"Yes, we do, to divorce court!" Shirley says.

They share more fun laughter.

"Have either of you dated a black guy before?" Helen asks.

"Gosh no," Mary responds rather quickly.

Shirley looks away and says, "Once, in college. A nice young man for about a year. It was nice."

"Just nice?" Helen asks.

"Nice, not enough sparks. How about you?" Shirley directs to Helen.

"Almost. It was supposed to be a double date before I met Davis, you all know Patty Hurston, well, she was going to set me up with her brother's friend; anyway, I couldn't do it. I wanted to try, but I just couldn't do it," Helen says.

"Your dad?" Shirley asks.

"Oh yeah! No way," Helen says.

They look away, smile, chuckle at times, then Mary breaks the moment.

"Have you decided about Amsterdam?" Mary directs to Shirley.

"I think I will go; it'll be fun. I've never been there. Either of you?"

"Twice," Helen says. "Once after college with a guy, then with Davis a few years ago. Great, romantic. We took train rides through Germany as well. You must do the trains."

"Beautiful in the country. I studied painting in a small village near the Amstel River for a month before dad got so sick. Be sure to rent a car. Study up before you go. Thomas is good about those kinds of things, isn't he?" Mary asks.

"Yes. He wants it to be business-pleasure. He loves driving around in new places. He mentioned something about France as well to visit a friend of Bruce's. But he's not sure," Shirley shares.

"How long?" Helen asks.

"Eight days. Two for business, the rest for fun!"

"The weather should be nice and mild, highs 70F to lows 50F," Mary says. "But check so you'll know what to take."

"I will, thanks," Shirley responds.

FIFTH

As Larry drove into town he thought of Rita. He wondered whether he should try to engage her in conversation or continue to listen when she speaks. They had been classmates, and though they were not friends, she too was usually at the top of the class in achievements. He remembered she had a brother and a couple of sisters and didn't think growing up anybody in their family was thought of as 'not right.' Her behavior now suggested schizophrenia, but since he was not a doctor he couldn't make a diagnosis. It was only odd that she knew things about him, and what course he was supposed to take. The talk of 'new dream,' and all that was beyond Larry's usual political involvement, though he had submitted a few short stories that had obvious political motive about race relations from his past experiences, 'positive experiences,' he thought. And he had written that paper freshman year of college about Dr. King. He couldn't see entirely past the fact that his present and past life had a meaning that was not intended by him, from street addict to esteemed counselor, hoodlum to good husband, good citizenship award to twice jailed. He understood that the past 28 years had allowed him to clear up the wreckage of his past, and help a lot of people get better, but there were still old things to make right. The incidents of the past few months were a bit unsettling and last night certainly was unexpected. Yet he was grateful that his skills for preservation were still tight and that when trouble found him, he could perform. Perhaps this was about a destiny he couldn't avoid, a purpose beyond his ability to steer. An unintended meaning because he was black, a meaning this country just couldn't shake. He hoped Rita had some answers for him.

He thought to drive past the bus stop to see if she was there, then turned right to go into the parking garage. He went up to his office and upon opening the door he saw an envelope on the floor. He picked it up, walked to his desk, sat, and opened it.

"Come see me, Rita."

He felt a chill throughout his body after he read the note. It seemed that forces beyond his control were again guiding him to participate in some adventure, something that was supposed to happen. He knew he wanted to end the groups and concentrate on assessments and individual sessions only but thought maybe he had a responsibility to the young folks, even though working with them kept his past life too fresh. On some level he wanted to disown it but knew that all those years of rough living had forever shaped his now.

###

He walked down the two flights of steps, went out the front door, and looked up the street to see if Rita was at her post.

Part of him didn't want to believe what was happening, yet he was going to trust it because this was his home area, and for whatever reason Rita had become his mentor.

"Good morning Larry," she greeted him. "I was deep in thought when you came by the last time."

Larry gestured to ask if he could sit, and she shook her head no.

"You are not a black man; you are a world man. Your life is not your own. The paper has a new dream. Get some crayons to scrub the missing words, blue and yellow. I will be away for a while. New dream. Tell them about the new dream. Be careful. More men will come. You need to get the device. Get a device soon."

Larry walked away, quickly now, with a sense of urgency to read the paper again. He had promised Darlene he would read it with her but as soon as he thought that Rita was behind him; "Your wife should not see it; she is not from the streets; she can help you, but she should not see it. That would change you. You must not change."

*

"So, who is this guy?" Bruce was asking his chief security officer.

"We don't know yet. We know he's very good with his hands. His military service was standard for the most part, he was a company clerk. However, he did have a temporary assignment for two weeks that was redacted from his records. We don't know what that was about."

"And last night?"

"He's very skilled. We could try again."

"Let it rest for a while," Bruce ordered.

###

Before going to prison Leroy ran with a rough crowd. They attended high school classes infrequently, bothered the girls when they attended, and showed off their intellects when given a chance, although briefly and with stage presence. It was a separation, not a collaboration. Leroy didn't know he was a leader but when he was busted by the feds there was a long list of violations upon decency and good order. A fifteen-year-old should not have been exposed to so much corruption so early in life. But Leroy loved the streets.

Jake Austin, on the other hand, was about as strait laced as they come, good student, good civilian, good young man. He was responsible, aware, and genial. He learned all that from his father who was a general clerk at the county courthouse before going back to school to get his law degree. He had maintained a small but prosperous real estate firm for forty years.

Jake and Marie Tolliver knew each other from high school but only dated after college and married within a year. They had three children two years apart as Jake set about his business career working as a manager in a manufacturing plant. He did well and went back to school at twenty-seven, completed a master's degree in business administration, and rose to VP of Operations.

He met Wallace Henson at a conference on Linear Programming as Henson was one of the presenters. Jake was impressed with the presentation and his ideas about using decision mathematics to establish production flow charts.

Oddly, Mr. Henson approached Jake after his lecture.

"I hear from my sources that you are familiar with silicon chip process and micro-processors," Wallace says surprising Jake early in their conversation.

"I've been at it a few years. I'm not an engineer though," Jake responds.

"I know plenty of them. I'm in need of someone to watch over my expanding business ventures," Mr. Henson offers. "Are you comfortable where you are or are you ready for new challenges?"

"I'm comfortable, but change can be good. What are you offering?" Jake asks, wary as he'd heard rumors about Henson's personal instability.

"I'm not that old but I can use some fresher eyes at the steering wheel as we're about to launch some new products."

"That's exciting!"

"How about if I get some information to you so you can see if you would be interested in joining us?"

"Sure, let me take a look," Jake answers.

"I'll send you an email with some non-proprietary projections as to where I think the industry is heading, and what we're looking at."

"Okay, sounds good."

"More than that, it is good! I'll be in touch."

"Okay. Good talking to you."

###

"Counselor, it's Rita. How are you this morning?"

"Not quite awake," he answers the phone.

"I hear you've retired. Have you given up on the new dream?"

"I thought I completed my work. I don't understand where the younger folks are now. Shouldn't someone else pick up the mantle?"

"You still have work to do. Post some more poems," she tells him.

"Okay," he said as Rita hung up.

*

"Double hearts swell when past sculptures tell
   a false regard for human passion
   minus the joy of love.
   Blue hearts must cover a broken vein of red
   coming back to freedom's will
   respecting all who care."

*

Rita's cancer had spread, and she was given no more than six months to live by her doctors. She had remained in good spirits during the last round of chemical therapy but last week decided to stop further attempts to prolong her life. She was fulfilled with a sense of freedom reaching out to the counselor one last time. She had a will drafted to turn her property over to him, and he could do whatever he wanted to with it. The house and land were now valued at $1.3 million dollars, and she had no surviving relatives. She appreciated the counselor fostering her notions of a new dream and they had accomplished much. He was a good counselor and friend to his clients and that was what the new dream was all about, helping those less fortunate. She had been struck by the fact that he had not treated her as some defective person speaking out of her mind when they reconnected, he treated her wishes with dignity and respect. She knew, however, there was one more task to complete, and Leroy would be involved.

###

Rita was not feeling well, and didn't know what to do with her feelings about Frankie D. He had harmed her in the worst way, but she had survived. She had told no one about the incident, and her parents had to go with the fact that she started calling herself Rita Bishop, that Rita Owens had died, starting in sixth grade following that afternoon she went missing. It was perplexing and her father had spent the better part of a month questioning kids in the neighborhood if they had seen, or knew anything about her disappearance that afternoon, but he got no answers. That new, haunting, straight ahead blank stare she developed afterwards was heart breaking, but everyone moved on, and she finished elementary and high school with no other problems.

It was only when she turned nineteen that people started describing her behavior as bizarre; she had never had a boyfriend, she was not able to hold a job, she would overdress for the seasons, and she walked around talking to herself. Occasionally she would hold a conversation with someone, but her range of knowledge and articulation was beyond most. Law, religion, philosophical inquiry, or historical facts and figures seemed to spew from her with a level of accuracy and depth that was considered special. Oddly, most of the time she would babble nonsense to the clouds. She was cared for however, and people made way to allow her to move about the small neighborhood of Dexter Village.

Rita had only seen Frankie once in the fifty-nine years since he molested her so seeing him last week stirred up feelings of anger about what he robbed her of. She was not cognizant of what it meant at the time, but she knew she had something to discuss with the counselor the next time she walked up on him.

*

Franklin Delaney was a year older than Rita and performed three other instances of sexual molestation before he turned fourteen, two other young girls and one effeminate young boy. As he started getting into trouble with the law and wound up in juvenile detention, he began to experience confusion about his own sexuality and had to use extreme discipline and fear not to act on certain urges. He began to get into fights and otherwise turned to violence to curb those dominant feelings. He had counseling while inside but was not able to develop a healthy sense of self and turned to drugs and alcohol when he got out. He spent time wandering the streets and at twenty was charged with attempted murder and sentenced to fifteen years in prison. He met Leroy at the state prison in Gainesville.

*

Leroy was tired of the brash new inmate talking loudly and taking advantage of the lesser endowed boys. During one particularly harsh screaming at, and punch to the face of a skinny kid Leroy rushed him from behind, grabbed his shoulders, and challenged him to a real fight. Frankie was surprised and before he could react Leroy slapped his face and threw him down to the floor, continuing to punch him until some other guys broke it up before the guards came in and placed the unit on lockdown.

"Who you dude?" Frankie asked. "Don't touch me again!" he shouted.

"Punk, don't you ever touch another soul in here unless you see me first, or I'll kick your ass some more! Punk!"

Frankie backed away but vowed to himself to do something to Leroy soon. He got his chance an hour later and Leroy was ready with a knife and a broom handle and beat Frankie about the head such that blood spewed forth and the guards and medic had to be called in. They attended his wounds but had to transfer him to a medical facility to control swelling and a large hematoma that developed on the side of his neck. Frankie passed out in the ambulance and CPR had to be performed to get him stable.

SEVENTH

Leroy, Celia, Larry, and Stephanie sat around the den discussing events of the day when Larry introduced the concept of time and what had occurred in their lives the past seven years. Of course, Larry and Stephanie had major grief issues as part of their individual stories and had only been seeing each other a few months. Celia and Leroy didn't have much outside of Leroy's business affairs and her painting and teaching; mundane or so they thought.

"You don't play around, do you?" Stephanie spoke up.

"It's just since I heard about the death of an old friend yesterday this whole life journey thing was given new meaning," Larry answered.

"Who?" Leroy asked.

"Marie Thomas, she was ninety. Did you ever meet her? Anyway, we worked together for years and had a social connection that was special as well. She would say I was born too late, that I reminded her of the 'Rat Pack' guys. That I had a swing and swagger that was appealing. She was from New Jersey and partied in New York, Vegas, and L.A. back in the fifties and sixties."

"And who did she say you reminded her of?" Celia asked.

"She never said, just that I was a cool, hip, sophisticated kind of guy. But that was a long time ago."

"You can be entertaining and fun loving," Stephanie chimed in. "What about the recent past though?"

"I'm not sure yet. It's been good times, but different challenges. The nature of my work changed a lot. The issues became tougher, and more dangerous. Clients were older and taking more risks; not fewer. These were people who knew how to be bad," Larry shared.

"This is at the federal level, right?" Celia asked.

"Yes," he answered. "But how about your work?" he asks Celia.

"Well, I think you're right, what I was painting years ago, and how I taught my students was different then; now there seems to be a need for edginess to evoke a kind of passion. I guess it's perspective, experiences, meanings. The world has changed so much. Of course, I don't have the same goals either," she referenced.

"Stephanie?" Celia gestures her way.

"I agree. I'm coming up on sixty and how I did what I did then seems miraculous looking back a decade ago. The cases, the workload, the energy, the consultations, I can't do all that now because of the complexities, legal and social. The definitions have changed, even though I'm still productive. What I retain about the cases has become different; I don't know what kind of results to expect. The state, as it were, may befriend my client without my knowing because they want a better deal than I was offering."

"Being run over?" Leroy asks.

"Yes, and not even being able to ride in the first place sometimes. Victimhood is so much more sophisticated now."

"How do you mean?" Leroy asked.

"Client to Judge: "Your honor, legal marijuana hurt my business, so I had to start dealing heroin, which was more profitable anyway." And the judge says, 'I understand,' and gives him a reduced sentence. And I had to accept it."

"More political?" Celia asks.

"More than you want to know. It's as if they want to kill off a certain segment of society."

"This is huge; let's revisit this?" Larry says.

"Sorry, back to your friend," Stephanie offers.

"Well, she was a classy lady, and when I first met her, I knew we would be friends, now this goes back thirty years. But something about the way we knew each other, I mean we didn't spend a lot of time together, but it was intimate."

"What do you think accounts for that?" Leroy asks.

"I think it was a combination of mother, sister, and some street allure. She was sophisticated for sure, but she had something else, a hidden depth, worldly in a civilized way, with no ill will towards anyone. We just talked, and laughed, and enjoyed good meals together."

"So, I suppose you both had depths unspoken to each other, but somehow perceived?"

"I think that's it, a knowing."

"Did Darlene know her?" Celia asks.

"She met her once I think; she knew I had this older, female friend who I met for lunch on occasion. Nothing more."

"You're pretty lucky," Stephanie spoke up. "Maybe I sense that in you as well, an unspoken depth."

"I think as we get older, we know right away who rode the bus, and who drove to school!"

###

Rita had been seen walking about the neighborhood, babbling to herself and having nonsensical interactions with people. She was taken in about a month ago for an evaluation at Avery Mental Institute and listed Larry Fleming as a contact. When they called him, he obliged and went in for a progress conference.

It had been three years since Larry had been inside the building. He had both bad and good memories from his time working there and felt unsteady about Rita's plight. It had been over a year since she contacted him, and they had a fabulous, clear conversation. She had implored him to continue to address the new dream and she was glad to talk to him again.

He entered the lobby and was greeted warmly by the receptionist who had worked the desk for fourteen years and knew of his contributions to the clinical setting. She was dressed comfortably with a crème-colored blouse, knit slacks and black flats. Not much makeup and a pair of gold earrings adorned her peach hued ear lobes. She was direct and professional.

"Yes, how may I help you, Mr. Fleming? Good to see you again."

"Thank you, Florence," he responded, not needing to read the name plate in front of her. "Good to see you as well. I'm here for a case Conference at two with Lindsey Baker, a social worker."

"Yes, she was just up here checking to see if you had arrived. I'll call her."

Within a few moments Ms. Baker was pushing open one of the electronically locked doors and signaled for him to come in. As he passed through, he heard the loud click of the large magnets being reconnected. Oddly, it put a smile on Larry's face.

He and Ms. Baker were not familiar, but she had been filled in by staff as to the eminence of Mr. Fleming and was told not to feel intimidated.

"Mr. Fleming, good to meet you. Thanks for coming to help your friend."

"Yes, she has had quite the course of experiences."

"Let's go into my office to chat a bit before meeting with her and the treatment team. Water, beverage of any kind?" she asked him.

"No thank you, I'm fine."

Her office was modest in size for a masters' level clinician, but comfortable enough for a small family conference or any one-on-one sessions. Her movements were direct and easy, but you could tell she wanted to set a certain tone for the conversation. She had only been at this for four years but had scored well in all clinical and performance reviews. She was good, but not hypervigilant. Her attire was teacher salary basic with a shallow upgrade. She was married with two young kids.

"Mr. Fleming, of course your reputation precedes you, so I will defer, when necessary," she begins.

"Well thank you but I will follow your leading and add where I can."

"Thank you, this is what we have."

Larry was patient as she took fifteen or so minutes to review all relevant permissions, and psych-social history information on Ms. Bishop. The only thing new to him was a reference to her being molested at eleven years old. At some point she had given the staff a name, but it had not been repeated by her. It seemed an obscure reference with no validity. Larry remained silent on that subject and asked about her behavior today.

"She's not well. She's been sitting in the day room talking to herself and moving if anyone tried to sit near her. She did not attend group or recreational therapy. She ate some of her breakfast, and her vitals are stable," the social worker relayed to him.

"What would you have me do?" Larry asked, curious that she had not mentioned Rita's terminal illness.

"She seems to cycle in and out of reality and we would like to make discharge plans but she's not socially stable at his time. We would hope seeing you resets her reality base. When she's lucid she speaks highly of you."

"So further back what's been happening?"

"Well, some days, or parts of days she babbles, and no one can understand what she's talking about, other times she's as clear as a professor on topic. Then she has her sleep over days where she stays in her room and sits in the chair for hours on end, then gets back in bed. Her hygiene suffers during those times."

"Ms. Baker, you've made no reference to her physical diagnosis," he says to her.

"Oh," she pauses and looks over some notes in the chart. "I don't follow you."

"Cancer, she has terminal Brain Cancer. She only has months to live."

"The intake assessment didn't include that, I'm afraid."

"And she's been here how long?" he asks her in a pointed way.

"I know where you're going, I have not done my job."

"Well of course any planning will have to include that. No notes from the attending physician?" Larry asks as he gets heated about this lapse.

"Mr. Fleming, I think I need to be excused," she asks of him, getting up from the chair and going down the hall to the nurse's station. "I'll be right back."

*

As he sat Larry, thought of the past and one of his first clients.

When Larry's mentor called, he could only tell him that the secret service would be involved, and he needed to be in his office by 7am Thursday morning, and that they would get there early, clean his office before and after the visit. Also, he would need to wear a suit and tie, shoes should be polished. Larry had been a certified addiction counselor only two years at that time. When she walked in security posted down the hall, not in front of the office door, and not in his office lobby. He would be alone with her for an hour.

She was tall, wearing pumps and a crisp linen suit, softly laced blouse, and no handbag. Her makeup was light, and she seemed to be about thirty-five years old. He recognized her right away, and did not reach out to shake her hand, she offered first, and he obliged.

"Mr. Fleming, Joy Winslip, my father sends his regards. He and Nelson are friends since college."

"Thank you, please sit down."

He gestures to the Queen Anne style love seat just beyond his desk, past the single chair. She sits and looks about the office. She seems uncomfortable and moves to the other chair, closer to him. He sits in his swivel and tries not to stare at her; she's gorgeous. She relaxes, crosses her legs, and begins a tale of drug abuse, crime, and a possible indictment. After an hour she asks to see him again next week, same time. He agrees. She gets up, thanks him, and leaves.

Larry quicky calls Mr. Nelson.

"Nelson, Larry. How are you this morning?" he asked his mentor.

"Fine, fine, thanks for calling. How are you?"

"Good, things are good. Ms. Winslip?"

"Okay, good, yes, you're learning. All I'm going to say is be yourself, strip away the excess, that's not your business. That's another world, stick to what you know. Be honest and listen more than talk."

"Okay. Thanks."

The next week she arrives, same as before, but this time a guard stands by the office door, outside in the hall. She takes a seat, and after pleasantries, she cries and starts to talk through the tears.

"How could I have been so stupid. I'm not a young woman, not a teenager. That bastard overdosed, I knew he wasn't strong enough, but the sex, you know, wild. So, he's smoking crack, and I'm shooting heroin, he passes out, drunk. Okay, so, I know, but anyway, I'm here, and they tried to get money from me, a lot. Man, those gang bangers are stupid. I pulled up with security, and they think they're going to rob me, stupid. Anyway, I've been clean a week and I'm okay. Oh, I did go to one of those meetings and it was good. I'm clean today. He didn't die, but he kept calling, I told him to go away. He has some pictures, but I'm not going to worry about that. I'm not the first one, right? I look good with clothes on or naked. Post them, I don't care. No money, bitch. So, you got any suggestions?"

"Do the next right thing."

"Okay, I'll see you next week."

*

Larry had his eyes closed and was in a deep meditative state when the social worker returned with his old friend Dr. Scott. They grinned a slow widening smile when Larry opened his eyes and saw the doctor. Lindsey Baker slowly retreated to a seat behind her desk as the doctor sat in the chair next to Larry.

"It's nice to see you Larry but this is a tough circumstance. The clinical lapse has been corrected and I offer my apologies," the doctor offers to his colleague.

"Thank you, sir. How is Ms. Bishop?" he asks, looking towards Ms. Baker.

"Mr. Fleming, it was a major oversight on my part. That will not happen again with another client of mine. And I appreciate Dr. Scott joining us."

"Yes, her situation is difficult, and we will keep her as comfortable as possible. It may be time for a hospice regimen, and we can do that here in the North Wing of the facility," Dr. Scott speaks up.

"Should we try for a visit today?" Larry asks.

"She is not coherent today, but if you would like to speak to her that would be fine."

"I would like to see her and for her to see me."

"Let's arrange that, in her room?" the doctor directs to Ms. Baker.

"She's out in the dayroom now and I will get her, and you can meet us there Mr. Fleming."

"I would prefer the larger room. Are many other clients there now?" he asks.

"No, about three," she responds and looks to Dr. Scott for guidance.

"I think that will be fine," doctor responds.

*

A copy of Larry's last book, The Moon Is My Confessor, was on a bookshelf in her office when Lindsey Baker came to work at Avery. She had read it and dismissed it as a good piece of fiction that didn't give her much insight into any psychiatric illnesses she had encountered up to that time. She thought it a nice thriller more appropriate for a prison population.

###

In closing, I long for the past, and yet, as history proves so far, the best is yet to come, here or in the great unknown!

George Harold Clowers, Jr.

One more thing.

AS TIME GOES BY

One of the more special aspects of living long is that we have a host of experiences to share with one another, hopefully mostly good, but just as well the not so good. I will make that judgement now as I'm dealing with the fact that a best friend from my teen years has died; he was seventy years old. The details of which don't matter now as I search my memory bank as to why this relationship has more meaning to my life than others I cherish, and what I come up with is that two young black boys in the late 1960's were able to attend an Atlanta Falcons Football game and not get harassed, dunk basketballs during warm-ups to the delight of the crowd, date twin sisters, and go to work with his father and ride in his dump truck on a few special Saturday mornings. We drank beers together as well and played on the varsity football team leading it to its first winning season in a number of years. Good, guy stuff!

Part of why I'm writing this is because of friendship, a mutual trust and support, born of an incident where a white teammate endured taunts during the game by an opponent who did not know the player's mother had recently passed so the vulgar taunts were truly demeaning, not just trash talking. Our friend didn't reciprocate during the game but when the buzzer blew he followed his nemesis to their locker room, and I couldn't let him go there by himself, so I followed, then my friend as well, and we gave our support. Justice was served, no one was badly hurt, and not a word was spoken of the event afterwards. A bond like no other, and that's what I'm feeling now, a bond like no other.

There are other aspects of growing up and living outsized experiences I could delve into but for the sake of this moment suffice it to say I am one of the lucky ones who has known long term connectedness through experiences that should have shattered any reason for us to have known, and maintained, that special bond. There are some things that just are, and too much analysis obscures the essence of knowing we make a difference to and in the world. Sweet journey my friend.

"Once you live a dream, and it is spent, it never returns; you hurt, but you never stop dreaming!"

Also by George Harold Clowers, Jr.

Addiction and the New Dream

Watch for more at www.georgeclowers.com.

About the Author

Retired substance use disorder counselor who worked at the highest levels.

He now writes poetry, short stories, and novels about his career.

Read more at www.georgeclowers.com.